MY SPECTACULAR SELF

Hammock for Two
An Empathy Story

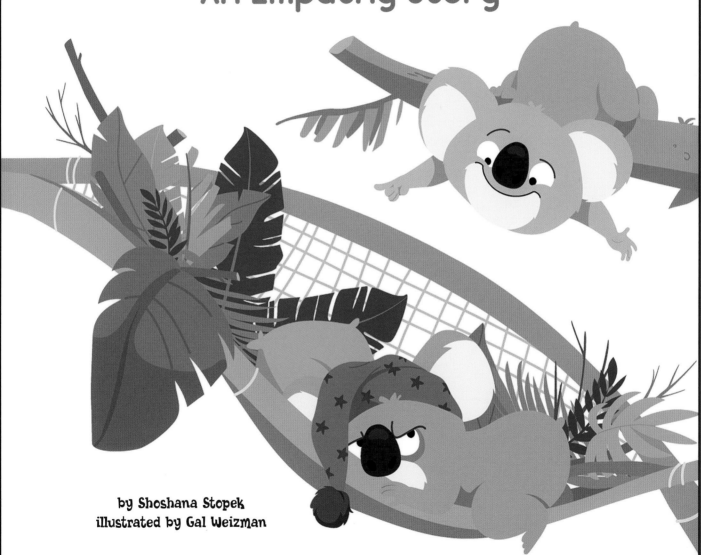

by Shoshana Stopek
illustrated by Gal Weizman

PICTURE WINDOW BOOKS
a capstone imprint

For Sasha, with love —S.S.

Published by Picture Window Books, an imprint of Capstone
1710 Roe Crest Drive, North Mankato, Minnesota 56003
capstonepub.com

Library of Congress Cataloging-in-Publication Data
Names: Stopek, Shoshana, author. | Weizman, Gal, illustrator.
Title: Hammock for two : an empathy story / by Shoshana Stopek ; illustrated by Gal Weizman.
Description: North Mankato, Minnesota : Picture Window Books, an imprint of Capstone, [2022] |
Series: My spectacular self | Audience: Ages 5-7. | Audience: Grades K-1. |
Summary: Sid the koala has found a new home with perfect trees, and a perfect hammock,
and he is ready to settle in for a long nap when he discovers he has an annoying neighbor,
Marvin, who really wants to be his friend—but when Marvin's hammock collapses Sid
realizes there is something more important than sleep.
Identifiers: LCCN 2021020814 (print) | LCCN 2021020815 (ebook) | ISBN 9781663984876
(hardcover) | ISBN 9781666332346 (paperback) | ISBN 9781666332353 (pdf) | ISBN 9781666332377
(kindle edition) Subjects: LCSH: Koala—Juvenile fiction. | Empathy—Juvenile fiction. |
Friendship—Juvenile fiction. | Conduct of life—Juvenile fiction. | CYAC: Koala—Fiction.
| Empathy—Fiction. | Friendship—Fiction. | Conduct of life—Fiction. Classification: LCC
PZ7.1.S7557 Ham 2022 (print) | LCC PZ7.1.S7557 (ebook) | DDC 813.6 [E]—dc23
LC record available at https://lccn.loc.gov/2021020814
LC ebook record available at https://lccn.loc.gov/2021020815

Special thanks to Amber Chandler for her consulting work.

Designed by Nathan Gassman

Meet Sid

HOBBIES: napping, meditating, reading

FAVORITE BOOKS: *The Art of Being Quiet* and *Koala Friends Forever*

FAVORITE FOODS: eucalyptus leaves, bark, and flowers

FUTURE GOALS: become a botanist who studies plants

GOALS FOR THIS YEAR:

* hang out in my new hammock

* make new friends
  (as long as they're not too loud)

* read new books

* more meditating

* more napping

Sid was looking forward to a nice, long nap in his new hammock. After a storm had destroyed his last home, Sid had found a perfect place to live that checked off everything on his list.

"Howdy, neighbor!" called a loud voice.
"I'm Marvin! What's your name?"

Please let this be a dream, thought Sid.

"I like your hammock," Marvin continued. "Does it fit two?"

"Hammock for ONE," mumbled Sid. He rolled onto his side, hoping his visitor would take the hint.

TAP! TAP!
BANG! BANG! PUH-CHING! PUH-CHING!

"Hey, neighbor!" called Marvin. "Look at us!
We're best friends already!"

Friends? thought Sid. That was definitely
NOT on his list.

Checklist for
the Perfect Home
✓ Shady tree
✓ Strong branch
✓ <u>NO NOISE
WHATSOEVER</u>

Sid gathered his belongings and was about
to storm off when he realized he did not
want to move again. And he REALLY
did not want to build another hammock.
And he REALLY, REALLY did want to nap.

So he climbed back into bed and closed his eyes . . .
until he felt something wet.

"Treats for two?" asked Marvin.

"I'm vegan," replied Sid.

Marvin nodded and left.

Moments later, Marvin returned. "A welcome gift!"

"Allergies," Sid sniffled.

Marvin tossed the flowers and disappeared again.

In a flash, he was back.

"Stuffies? They are very cuddly."

"Personal space," Sid replied.

Sid was pretty sure this was getting a bit weird.

Nevertheless, Marvin kept offering little gifts.

"Dairy-free munchies?"

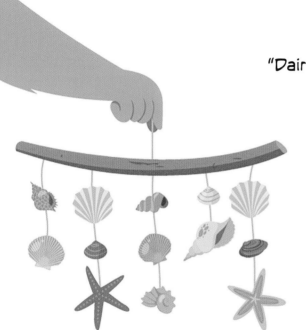

"A mobile made out of seashells?"

"All my favorite books?"

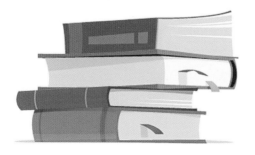

"A reading lamp that doubles as a night–light?"

"A prickly plant?"

"How about a sun hat?"

Just when Sid thought things couldn't get any stranger,
Marvin brought in the BIG gifts.

"Room décor?"

"A computer?"

"Bookcase?"

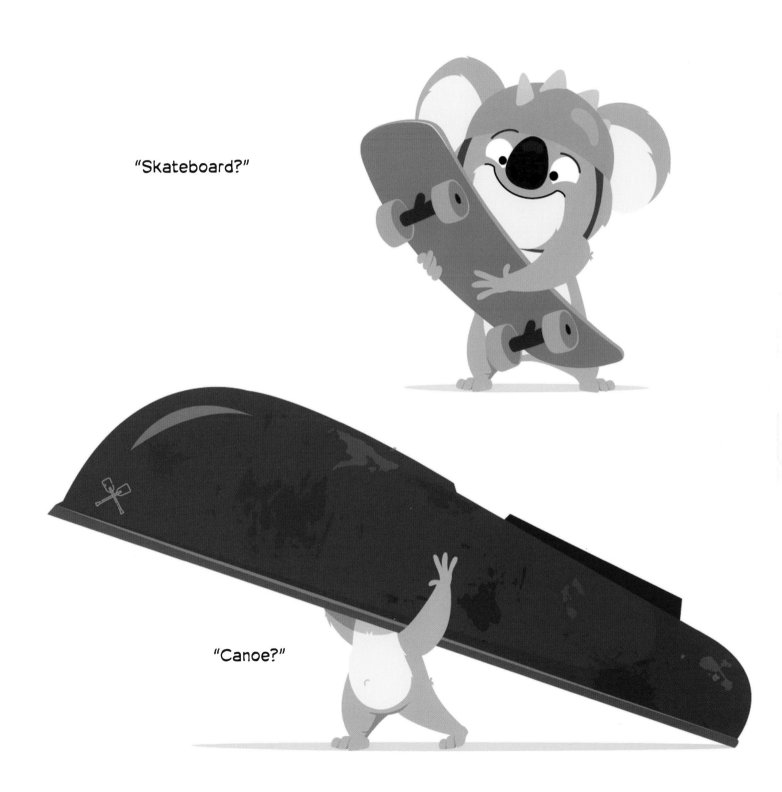

"Skateboard?"

"Canoe?"

The gifts really began to stack up.

Finally, Marvin appeared with a large wooden box.

"A foot stool that doubles as a chest for your blankets!"

"That's IT!" exclaimed Sid. "I don't need a foot stool or a plant or a bookcase or a canoe or anything else from you! All I NEED is some peace and quiet so I can just take a nap."

Sid had a feeling he had gone too far, but he couldn't stop himself. He had reached his limit.

Apparently, Marvin's hammock had reached its limit
as well. It began to buckle under the weight of all
the unwanted gifts.

The knots untethered, and the hammock broke free
from the branch. It plunged toward the ground
and landed with an enormous **THUD!**

For the first time, there was silence.

"Uh, Marvin?" Sid called. "Are you okay?"

Sid climbed down the tree to check on Marvin.

"I just wanted to be your friend," said Marvin, sadly.
"And now I've lost my home."

Suddenly, Sid understood how Marvin felt. He remembered when his hammock had been destroyed and how sad he had been. He could tell that Marvin was feeling the same way now.

Sid realized that he wanted to help Marvin. And maybe, just maybe, Sid could use a friend after all!

It had been quite the day, and Sid was looking forward
to a nice, long nap in his hammock with his new friend—
even if it wasn't as quiet or peaceful as he was used to.

Show Empathy

Empathy is being able to understand how someone else feels. Here are some great reminders of ways to show empathy to your friends.

listen

consider others first

be supportive

encourage

try to understand

be helpful

respect feelings

be kind

imagine how they feel

Empathy Matters

1. Have you ever had something important to you break or not work anymore? How did that feel?

2. When Sid is trying to be alone, he is bothered by Marvin. Do you ever feel annoyed when you want to be alone and someone bothers you? Is there a nice way to say you'd like to be alone?

3. What does an annoyed face look like? What does a sad face look like? If you were Sid, which face would you make? If you were Marvin, which face would you make?

4. Marvin tries very hard to be Sid's friend. How can you try to be a friend?

5. What lesson do you think Sid learns? What lesson do you think Marvin learns?

About the Author

Shoshana Stopek is the author of numerous books for kids and grown-ups. Her picture book series My Spectacular Self includes *Hammock for Two, Out-of-Control Rhino, Heads Up!,* and *Sometimes Cows Wear Polka Dots*. Shoshana grew up in New Jersey, where she learned how to make new friends, fly a kite, and bedazzle a wardrobe. Now she lives in Los Angeles with her husband and daughter where she writes and occasionally still bedazzles. Visit her at shoshanastopek.com.

About the Illustrator

Gal Welzman was born in Jerusalem, dreaming of flying above the white stone houses of her neighborhood like Peter Pan. As she grew older and became more acquainted with the laws of gravity, she had to abandon that plan. Instead, she devised a different way to never grow up: she attended Bezalel Academy of Arts and learned to draw. Gal loves to illustrate animals and creatures and to see her creations come to life. Her illustrations are bouncing through games and TV shows, sitting on packaging, and living in various children's books around the globe.